ACCIDENTALLY AWESOME!

WRITTEN BY
ADAM WALLACE

ILLUSTRATED BY
JAMES HART

D0039766

KRUEGER WALLACE
PRESS

ACCIDENTALLY AWESOME!

First published in the year of the werewolf, 2015
Published by Krueger Wallace Press
6/155 Lower Heidelberg Rd
Ivanhoe East   VIC   3079
Australia
Email: wally@adam-wallace-books.com or visit
www.adam-wallace-books.com

Editor: Tex Calahoon

Designer/Typesetter: James Hart
Printed in Australia by McPherson's Printing Group
ISBN: 978-0-9808282-7-6
Text copyright © Adam Wallace 2014
Illustrations and cover copyright © James Hart 2014

Cataloguing-In-Publication entry is available
from the National Library of Australia
http://catalogue.nla.gov.au

Do not stick this book up your nose.
This book is not a golf club or a tasty pudding.

This book is for all the awesome kids who road-tested it and gave me advice. Even though you made me cry a little bit, I got over it and now I think this is a better story because of your suggestions.

CHAPTER ONE

I'm always in the right place at the right time. At least, that's what everyone keeps telling me.

'Jackson, you're always in the right place at the right time. You're a true hero.'

That's what they say, and let me give you a couple of examples of why they say it. What this will show you is that while they all *think* I'm a big hero, I'm actually just a big fluke!

Tuesday 20th May. I was riding my bike down the steepest hill near my house. It is so awesome to ride down, although it's **MASSIVELY** scary too. I think that's what makes it fun. Anyway, I was flying down the hill when I heard a woman scream.

2

I didn't know what was going on so I slammed on my brakes and I skidded ... and skidded ... and skidded (*well I had been going fast!*) ... skidded some more ... almost lost it ... just missed a pothole ... skidded ... shut my eyes ... skidded ... hit a kerb ... flipped over the handlebars ... squealed like a little baby ... waited for the owies and ouchies ... hit a guy running along the footpath ... head butted him with my helmet ... landed softly on his big gut then stood up, shaken but not stirred. The guy was out cold. There was a handbag on the ground next to him.

3

It was Mrs Watson's. She ran up, breathing hard after her 20m run. She's pretty old.

'Oh, Jackson.' She has this real posh-lady voice. 'Oh, Jackson dahling, you rahlly were in the right place at the right time. The way you jumped off your bike to tackle that robber was simply divine and *SOoo* brave. You are my hero.'

She called the cops, who came and took the guy away. They said he'd done it before, but they couldn't catch him. They patted me on the head and said well done. That pat on the head was my reward for doing what the entire police force couldn't get done. Whoopadee doo.

Friday 23rd May. Mum gave me $10 to go and buy some milk. She said I could use the change to get something for myself. So here's the thing. Our milk bar does

4

the best mixed lollies ever … **EVER!** But, they also do a pretty mean milkshake, and I was kinda busting for a milkshake. What to do?

I got to the milk bar and Toby, the guy who worked there, was about to put up a poster because his cat had gone missing.

'Hi Jackson,' he said, and he was really sad. 'Joolsy is gone. I wish you could help me find him.'

I smiled and said I hoped he found the cat. I was really thinking about whether to get a milkshake or lollies, so I was distracted when I opened the door to the fridge and, without really looking, I reached in and grabbed ... a cat's face.

I knew it was a cat's face because the whiskers tickled my hand and it meowed. I let it go real fast and it leapt onto my head. It was shaking, probably because it was freezing in that fridge.

'Oh Jackson,' Toby shouted, pulling the cat off my head. 'You found Joolsy. I've been looking everywhere for him. I was just about to set a reward, but now I don't need to. You were in the right place at the right time. You really are a hero.'

I paid for the milk and went home, still a bit shocked at having grabbed a cat in the face. It was only when I got home that I realised I hadn't got a milkshake *or* mixed lollies

and, even worse, there had been enough change to get both.

See? I'm a hero, but I'm over it. I don't want to be in the right place at the right time. I can't handle it any more. I'm only 11, and I feel like I'm cheating everyone, because everything I do is by accident. One day, they'll all realise that too, and they'll hate me. So I'm done. I'm quitting. But how do you quit being a fluke?

CHAPTER TWO

Step one in my plan was to try and avoid trouble hotspots. Step one in my plan didn't work. I went to the nursing home to visit my Grandpa (my mum's dad). I do that sometimes, because Grandpa likes the company and I like the smell of old people. It was surely one place that wouldn't need a hero … or so I thought.

I sat with Grandpa while he ate some mashed corn. We were watching the soaps on TV, which was what the old ladies wanted to watch.

Grandpa couldn't get angry and ask them to change it or his false teeth would fly out. That would have been pretty funny, except for the fact that every time Grandpa's false teeth fly out, I have to pick them up and give them back to him. What *that* means is that I get Grandpa slobber and mashed corn on my hand.

Anyway, I was sitting with Grandpa when Mrs Spinsy came "running" into the room. I say "running" because it took her five minutes to get the ten metres from the door to us.

'Oh Jackson,' she said. 'It's so good to see you. You're a good boy, Jacks-oh no.'

The oh no was because her teeth flew out and landed in Grandpa's mashed corn. He picked them up and tried to put them in his mouth. He was distracted by the television. I reached over and took them off him, meaning my hand was covered in Grandpa slobber, mashed corn, **and** Mrs Spinsy slobber. I gave them back to Mrs Spinsy, and then we were surrounded by old people. They all wanted to say hello to me. I don't think they got many visitors.

All five Beryls were there, and so were three Joans, four Harrys, five Pams and two Williams.

I stood up to say hello, tripped over a walking frame, fell flat on my face and knocked a walking stick out of the hand of one of the Williams. It went up in the air, flipped a couple of times then hit the TV and changed the channel. William fell onto a beanbag.

'Hey, I was watching that!' cried Grandpa, his false teeth flipping into his cup of warm milk.

Suddenly all the old people started yelling about what show they wanted to watch. I got off the ground and saw that

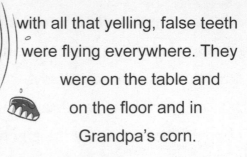

with all that yelling, false teeth
were flying everywhere. They
were on the table and
on the floor and in
Grandpa's corn.

I sighed and knew I
should help. I picked up all
the teeth, meaning I had slobber
and bits of old boiled lollies all
over my hands. As I went to put
the teeth on the table, I kicked
William's walking stick, which was
still on the ground.

The stick hit the TV, changing
the channel again. The teeth flew into
the air. I caught the first two
pairs, groaning as some fruit
cake squished between my fingers.

Then there were too many teeth. I threw up the ones I had so I could catch the others, and suddenly I was juggling eight pairs of teeth! Everyone clapped. I wasn't really juggling, I just did **NOT** want to hold those teeth firmly, so I kept throwing them up and catching them.

I couldn't do it forever, though. I tripped on a pair of slippers. The teeth flew in all directions. The old people gasped, meaning their mouths were open ... and a set of teeth flew into each mouth!

I didn't know if they were the right teeth for the right people, but they didn't care. Grandpa went back to watching the soaps, and all the old ladies came up to give me a thankyou kiss on the cheek.

I sat there and took the kisses. I ignored the old lady beards scratching my cheek.

I ignored the old lady slobber and bits of scotch-finger biscuit dribbling down my face. I just sat there, wishing as hard as I could that I would stop being awesome by accident all the time.

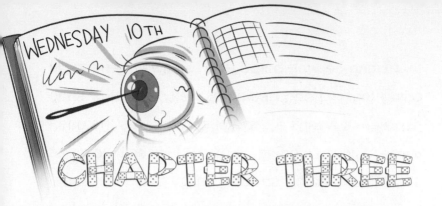

CHAPTER THREE

It all changed on a Wednesday. I would never have guessed it would be on a Wednesday. If I tell the absolute no-lie stick a needle in my eye truth, I never expected it to happen at all. And even if it did, it should have happened on some exciting day like a Saturday. Still, as I said a second ago - or a minute ago, depending on how fast you can read - it was on a Wednesday.

I was riding home from school, and I was going pretty slow. It had been a long day, and I just wanted to cruise home.

Then I heard someone shout out, **'HELLLLLP! I'M GOING TOO FAST!!!'**

I looked around and saw Matthew Wiley riding down the hill in a shopping trolley. He did that when he was bored, but he always ended up going too fast and getting scared. I made a snap decision. It wasn't a good one, but it was the one I made. I wasn't going to help. I wasn't going to cheat Matthew by saving him by accident. Then, because I was watching him as I rode, I crashed straight into a fire hydrant, flipped over the handlebars, and ended up on my butt on the nature strip. My bike wobbled backwards out onto the street.

I watched as Matthew and the trolley

16

whizzed down the hill, haha whizz, and then I watched as the trolley hit my bike, flew into the air, landed, rolled, and crashed into Mr Parker's BMW.

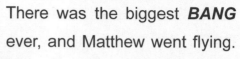

There was the biggest **BANG** ever, and Matthew went flying. Luckily, he landed in a bush. Unluckily, it was a rose bush. Luckily, his fall was cushioned. Unluckily, his fall was cushioned by heaps of really sharp rose thorns. Matthew screamed, ran around in circles, then sat on the grass sucking his thumb. Mr and Mrs Parker ran outside to see what had happened.

'My car! My beautiful car!' Mr Parker shouted. He ran around in circles, then sat on the grass sucking his thumb.

'It was Jackson's fault!' wailed Matthew, the little rat. 'Jackson made me crash!'

Mr Parker glared at me.

I couldn't believe it. He didn't even give me a chance to explain, just because Matthew's dad was his really rich boss. Also, I couldn't take him seriously because he was still sucking his thumb like a baby. Then he took it out and spoke.

'Well, you were in the wrong place at the wrong time, Jackson,' he said through gritted teeth.

'Yeah, Jackson,' said Matthew, still bawling. 'You were in the wrong place at the wrong time.'

Then he cried his way up the street to his house.

Mr Parker looked at me.

'I think you'd better go home,' he said. 'I don't want to do something I might regret.'

What, like sucking your thumb like a baby, because you already did that, I thought, but decided not to say anything.

I was happy to get out of there, but I did feel pretty strange. Usually, I was in the right place at the right time to stop bad things happening. This time, I hadn't tried to help and it meant I was in the **wrong** place at the **wrong** time. Or the right place at the right time, but stopping Matthew's wild ride had made a **bad** thing happen. I had stopped helping and I had stopped being a hero. It was only the next day I would find out how true that actually was.

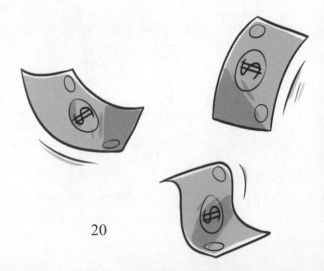

20

CHAPTER FOUR

Thursday was all downhill. First, I rode my bike up the hill to school with Johnny, my best friend (*more about him later!*). So maybe Thursday was uphill and then downhill.

Anyway.

I was about to put my bike on the stand when Rosie Maloney put her bike in the spot next to me. Her bike started to fall. I didn't help, sticking to my plan. I just kept pushing my bike forward. Then the big bad started. Rosie's bike hit the ground. As she reached for it, I ran over her long, long hair with my bike tyre. She screamed. I jumped ... and my bike hit her in the face. She had a blood nose and everything.

She yelled at me for not helping, but she was holding her nose and it made her voice sound funny, and I couldn't help laughing. That made her madder! She ran off, but couldn't see properly because of the nose and the blood and the hair, and she ran straight into a tree.

I helped her then by walking her to First Aid. Then things got *really* bad!

At recess, I threw my banana peel at the bin, but it missed and landed on the ground ... just as my teacher, Mr Teetee, walked past. I got worried and leant down to pick it up ... so did Mr Teetee, and we did a massive head butt. My head is pretty hard and Mr Teetee wobbled, slipped on the banana peel, and fell face-first into the sandpit right where little Anthony, the youngest kid in school, had just done a wee. So the sand was wet ... and yellow.

Mr Teetee glared at me and went to clean himself up. Things had changed, alright.

At lunchtime, instead of having lunch with Johnny, I went down to the back of the oval by myself. I leant on a tree, just as a bird flew behind me.

I squashed it against the tree! It wasn't happy and pecked me right on the ear. This was crazy. I kept being in the wrong place at the wrong time, and it got even worse on the way home. I had to go to the bank because Mum asked me to bank a cheque for her beauty salon. It was her business, and she would normally have done it, but was giving a man a cure or something. I don't know how sick he was, or why he went to a beauty salon and not a doctor.

Anyway, I rode to the bank and parked my bike. Our bank had only been robbed one time in like a hundred years, and I had stopped it by opening the door as the robber ran towards it. The door hit him square in the face and knocked him out. I had been a hero.

Not today.

I heard a cry for help, but I ignored it. This time when I opened the door, a different robber was running out of the bank, but I didn't open it at the right time. He was still a metre away from it, and he just ran straight through.

'Thanks kid!' he yelled. 'You're a great help.'

He may have thought so, but the

bank manager and customers and
police and everyone else didn't agree.
They all glared at me, shaking their heads. It was
like, in an instant, they forgot all the times I had
helped. I tell you what, it was the worst day of my
life. Helping people by total fluke was way better
than being a total anti-hero who hurt people and
squashed birds and who everyone hated.

It seemed like I had two choices. Either I could use my accidentalness to become a super evil villain, or I had to figure out how to turn things around and get my hero-ness back. Not a hard choice really. I didn't want to be a villain no one liked who would end up having to live in a secret lair all on my own and where I would have to cook my own dinner. Besides that, I *wanted* to be good. I actually *liked* helping people. It was time to go back to using my flukiness for good and not evil!

CHAPTER FIVE

Phase one of my plan. Make it happen. *I* had to make it happen. I had to be in the right place at the right time. I figured the only way to do that was to set up some bad stuff, pass by at just the right time, and stop it. It was, if I do say so myself, pure genius. A little evil and sneaky maybe, but pure genius just the same. In fact, I was so happy at having thought of such a cool idea I went and made myself an ice-cream sandwich.

After I finished my sandwich, I wiped my face clean and got to work. I needed a time, a place, and an event. I decided on Saturday, around mid-morning. That way I could have a sleep-in and still have time to set everything up.

27

Now for a place. I needed somewhere pretty public, so that everybody would be able to see I was back in business. Aha. The market. That would be **perfect**.

Everybody went to the market on Saturdays to get their fresh fruit and vegetables. I always went for a sausage in bread. Man, I love a good sausage in bread.

So that was a time and a place sorted. The tricky part was thinking of a setup that didn't **look** set up. An accident, or a crime, or … **JACKPOT!!!** I was staring out the window and I saw the bank robber. **Seriously!** I couldn't believe he would be so stupid as to hang around after robbing a bank. But there he was, just wandering down the street.

I raced out the front door and skidded to a stop in front of him. It was the guy from the bank alright, although his nose was shorter and he had less hair and he had a limp and he was about ten centimetres taller. Just your basic disguise, really.

'Hey,' I said, 'I know you.'

He looked at me a bit weirdly, and he took a step back. I guess he was worried I was going to dob him in.

'It's okay,' I said. 'I'm not going to dob you in. I like the disguise by the way.'

He looked at me, as if he was trying to read my mind. Then, suddenly, he recognised me.

'The kid from the bank. You really helped me out, kid. But this ain't no disguise.'

'Yeah right,' I said, and I reached up to pull his nose out to its true length. He cried out in pain.

'OW! I was wearing the disguise at the bank, kid! Sheesh.'

29

Whoops. I let go of his nose and wiped my hand on my jeans. I had to move on with my plan anyway.

'I want to help you out again,' I said.

He looked at me, waiting to hear what I was going to say.

'At the market, on Saturday mornings, Mr Popadopolus always sells out of cupcakes by 10:15. At 10:30 exactly, every market, he closes up his stall, puts his huge wad of cash in a zip-up bag, walks through the market then goes into a dark alley. Halfway down the alley he gives the money to his nephew, who takes it to the bank. You could rob him just before he turns into the alley. You could get *all* his money!'

The bank robber looked at me like it was a trick.

'Everyone will see me rob him if I do it before the alley. Why don't I wait until he goes down it? Then I'll be hidden.'

I rolled my eyes like it was obvious.

30

'Because halfway down the alley is the secret handover point to the nephew, George, who is a weightlifting muscle man karate star. He will beat the living snot out of you.

He's a slow runner, though, so if you do it at the start of the alley, George will never catch you. Neither will Mr Popadopoulus. He's 70. He might break a hip.'
I felt bad for Mr Popadopoulus, but there were bigger things at stake here. Like my reputation.

'I'll create a distraction,' I said, playing my trump card. 'Everyone will look at me and you can snatch the bag and get away.'

My plan, of course, was to create a distraction and then use my accidental awesomeness to stop the robber. It was brilliant.

Nothing could go wrong. The robber nodded.

'Alright kid, you seem like you're for real, although I don't know why. Do you want a slice of the pie or something?'

I do like pie, but I knew he really meant the money, so I shook my head.

'No. I just like helping people, and robbers are people too.'

The robber looked a little sad.

'We are kid, we really are. If only other people understood us like you do.'

Yeah right, I thought, *I'm just using you, you robber creepo. You actually totally freak me out.* I went back into plan mode.

'See you on Saturday then,' I said cheerfully. 'Don't be late. Mr Popadopoulus never is.'

The robber nodded and walked off, and phase one was complete!

CHAPTER SIX

Phase two. Saturday morning.

I rode my bike to the market early, telling mum and dad I wanted a sausage. They weren't surprised.

I checked the market out and it all seemed normal enough. People getting fruit and vegies. Butchers yelling out specials. The drunken hobo on the corner yelling stuff I couldn't understand.

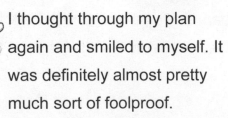

I thought through my plan again and smiled to myself. It was definitely almost pretty much sort of foolproof.

I decided to go and get one sausage.

At 10 o'clock, after my third sausage, I wandered over towards Mr Popadopoulus's stall to see how he was going. He sold the best cupcakes ever, which was why he always sold out early. As I got closer, though, I sensed something was wrong. There were still quite a few cupcakes left. I looked at Mr Popadopoulus. He had huge muscles and wasn't 70. *Oh no*! It was George. I went up to the stall.

'Where's Mr Popadopoulus?' I asked, my voice screechier than usual.

'He bit sick,' George explained in his thick accent. 'So I am do stall. My wife, she take money to car. But sell slow today.'

He looked sad. So did I. Not only was George's wife super fast, she was also a champion wrestler. The robber was in for a hard time. I realised George was still talking.

'My wife, she not so good neither. She has
broken leg, so on crutches. It will be
slow walk to car for her, and
she go all the way, I must clean
stall tip to top for Papa.'

I nodded. Oh boy, this wasn't
good. At 10:15 there were still
seven cupcakes left. This was the
time they were usually all gone, and
Mr Popadopoulus would start
counting and sorting all the money.

I checked my wallet, but I only had enough for three cupcakes. I bought those, and wondered what to do next. I realised there was only one choice. I moved to the front of the stall and started yelling.

'Get your cupcakes here. World famous super dooper cupcakes! You know you want 'em, only four left, get in quick before they're all gone.'

One cupcake sold straight away. Still three left. I tried harder.

'Come on, people, Mr Popadopoulus is sick. Help out an old man so he can buy some special medicine.'

That wasn't a totally made-up story. I assumed he would need medicine. Either way, I sold the last three and helped George count and sort all the money. He was very glad for my help.

'You good boy, Jackson, not bad like people say.'

Yeah, yeah, keep counting, Muscles. Finally, at 10:29, the money was ready. One minute to go. I saw the robber hanging around the alley. George's wife got on her crutches and started walking with the money through the market. I pointed at her. The robber nodded.

Suddenly, I realised I hadn't thought of a distraction. I looked at the cupcakes in my hand. I threw one at the back of the head of the last person who had bought one.

It was my Nan (my dad's mum),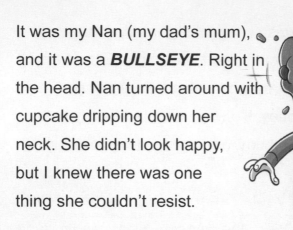
and it was a **BULLSEYE**. Right in
the head. Nan turned around with
cupcake dripping down her
neck. She didn't look happy,
but I knew there was one
thing she couldn't resist.

FOOD FIGHT!

Nan smiled and
threw her cupcake at
me, but I was ready. I
ducked, and it hit Mr
Teetee right on the end
of his nose and stayed there.
He pulled it off. Meanwhile, the

people who had bought cream pies and Boston buns were looking edgy. *Come on*, I thought, *do it, I need you*. They did it. A cream pie hurled through the air and hit me in the face.

AWESOME!

George's wife was almost at the alley. I threw another cupcake and hit a lady right on the ear. She reached into her bag, pulled out a mango, and threw it.

It was all on. Food was flying everywhere. Someone got hit on the ear with a rump steak. Someone got hit in the face with a frozen yoghurt cone. Someone got hit in the butt with a watermelon.

I got closer to the robber. Just as he was about to snatch the money I hurled my last cupcake, hoping to knock him off balance and draw attention to what he was doing. I would be a hero.

Unfortunately, just as I was about to release, I got hit in the side of the head by a flying lettuce. It knocked me off balance and the cupcake hit George's wife in the side of the face. She cried out, wobbled on her crutches, and dropped the money right into the robber's hands. He laughed out loud.

George's wife was off-balance now. Her crutch swung around and hit a guy between the legs, making him drop his bag of fruit. George's wife stood on a banana with her good leg and flew into the air before landing really hard on the ground. I found out later she broke a bone in her butt.

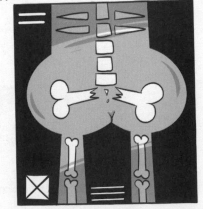

40

'Thanks again, kid!' the robber called out. He waved the money bag and ran off. I stood frozen, looking at the chaos around me. Then I saw George. He was walking towards me. He was not happy. It looked like the big vein in his head was about to pop.

'You bad kid, Jackson, like everyone say. I no happy now!'

Oh no. Everyone thought I had set up the whole robbery. Which I guess I had. There was only one thing to do. **RUN AWAY**! I bolted down the alley and through the car park to my bike. I jumped on and rode off at full speed. I got about 4 metres before my chain broke.

I flipped over the handlebars and belly flopped onto the bonnet of Mr Parker's newly fixed shiny BMW.

I dented it again.

I sat up and saw I was surrounded. The crowd closed in. My bad luck was now the worst luck.

Uh oh.

CHAPTER SEVEN

Suddenly I heard screeching tyres. I looked up and there was Nan in her little old lady car. I had never been so glad to see it. She skidded to a stop in front of the crowd, blocking them off, and opened the passenger side door.

GET IN, JACKSON!

43

I opened the back door, threw my bike in the back seat, then jumped in the front. Everyone was yelling at me, but Nan sped off ... well, she drove off pretty fast for an old lady, which was actually just a teeny bit faster than people can run, and the yelling crowd gave up after they realised they were very unfit.

Nan said she would drive me home, but she didn't. She stopped at a park and we went and sat on the swings. I know, you probably can't imagine a Nan sitting on a swing, but my Nan is really cool.

'What's going on, Jackson?' she asked. 'That was pretty strange there today.'

I nodded, but couldn't think of what to say. Nan squished a cake on the side of my head.

'Talk to me, Jackson. You can always talk to me. You know that.'

44

I knew. So I wiped the cake off my face, ate the icing, and then I told Nan everything. I hadn't meant to, but it all came blurting out. How people expected me to be responsible for saving everything. How they thought I was great when I was actually a total fluke, a cheat, a fake. How I had suddenly become the exact opposite of awesome, and was now an accidental villain. How I had tried to fix things, but had made things worse. I was letting everyone down and they hated me.

As if to prove it, just at that second a guy drove past and yelled out his window, 'You're letting everyone down and I hate you!'

I groaned. How mean was that? I just wanted to be back to normal, a trouble saver not a trouble maker.

Finally, when I finished, Nan opened her eyes. I hoped she had been concentrating and not taking a nanna nap.

'You know what?' she said. 'When I was younger, I always wanted to fall in love and get married.'

I didn't mean to, but I stuck my tongue out, did a gagging noise, and pretended to be sick. It was my natural reaction whenever people talked about kissy kissy love stuff. Nan ignored me and kept talking.

'I did everything the other girls did, but I wasn't being myself. I went to picnics I thought were boring, and I talked about things I thought were boring. I tried to force it to happen, but it never did. Not until I went back to being myself. Do you understand what I am saying?'

I shook my head. I had no idea what this had to do with me being awesome again. Did she want me to get married or something? I was only 11. Nan sighed.

'Okay,' she said. 'Now listen closely and try and keep up. Read between the lines. If a lion eats monkey food, that doesn't make him a monkey. Get it?'

'But I like monkeys, Nan. They're so cute.'

Nan slapped her forehead.

'Okay,' she said, 'how about this. Do you understand what I mean when I say be as thou art, as thou art a thing of beauty?'

She may as well have been speaking in gobbledygook, although it was nice she called me beautiful. Actually, I think I would have preferred handsome. I hoped she had taken the right pills. I gave the only answer that came into my head.

'Gah?'

Nan rolled her eyes and tried again.

'Be grateful for what you have.'

I didn't have any more cupcakes. I would have liked another one. I stared at Nan. I was getting confused and going cross-eyed. She sighed and went into overdrive.

'When life gives you lemons, you can make lemonade. See? It's a piece of cake.'

I had never had lemonade cake before, but it sounded nice.

'Do you understand me now?' she asked.

I shook my head.

'This is harder than I thought,' Nan sighed.

48

'Okay. No more reading between the lines, I'll say it straight out. Be yourself, Jackson. Let the situations happen, don't force them. Once you're grateful for the gift you have, once you help others for the sake of helping, things will return to normal, I promise.'

I shrugged, indicating I still wasn't getting it.

'Don't try so hard to be someone you're not,' Nan said.

'Sorry Nan, not with you.'

Nan rubbed her temples but kept trying.

'Let the luck come naturally.'

'Nope, it's not getting through to me.'

She stared at me for a second.

'You're a dull boy, Jackson.'

Nan got off the swing and walked to her car. She threw my bike onto the grass and screeched her tyres as she drove off. I stayed on the swing, wondering if we had any lemonade at home.

CHAPTER EIGHT

That night, I had a dream. In the dream, a monkey was picking nits out of Nan's hair and eating them, the sun was actually a giant cupcake wearing sunglasses, and I was in a bag of lemons. Then the bag tipped me out and the sunny cupcake spoke to me in a voice that sounded like a ghost.

'Jackson. *JACKSON!* Be grateful for your heroic skills. Luck doesn't matter. All that matters is helping others. The helping is its own reward. Let the luck come naturally. Do not try to force it.'

Then it fell out of the sky and landed on my head. I woke up and really *did* have cupcake all over my face. I need to stop eating half my supper

in bed and leaving the rest for later. But I knew what I had to do! The freaky weird dream cupcake had told me. Helping people was the right thing to do, and because I wanted to help, not just because I was expected to. *How* I helped them didn't matter, as long as I helped, so my luckiness was actually a good thing, not a bad thing! And if I could help people and feel good about it, a reward would just be a bonus. It was like a huge weight had been lifted off my shoulders.

Thank you, giant sun cupcake!!!

FARRRT!!
FART!!

I showered, dressed, ate breakfast, fixed my bike chain, and rode to Johnny's house.

Like I said before, Johnny's my best friend. We always ride to school together, sit next to each other in class, and Johnny always makes me laugh. Pretty much every teacher we have ever had has said to us at some stage, 'You two should *not* be sitting together.'

Every Sunday, Johnny's parents make him go to church with them and then go home for Sunday lunch. It's their family day. Still, they always said I could go over any time, and Johnny liked me going on Sundays because it got him out of the house for a little bit.

I was too eager though. I got there at 10:30. They weren't home from church yet. I rode up and down the street a couple of times, but I was **bored bored *BORED!*** I tried bunny hopping over the kerb but hit it and flipped over the handlebars. I *hate* bunny hops. They are so the stupidest things ever, even more stupid than ... my thought stopped right there. From my position lying on the ground, I could see Johnny's house. I could see the house, the windows, the door, and I could see that someone else knew that Sunday was church time for Johnny and his family.

Climbing out of the top floor window was ... *the robber from the bank and the market!* And now he was robbing my best friend's house! He had a bag over his shoulder, and it looked full. There was a ladder against the wall, and he started climbing down it. He went slowly, so the bag must have been heavy.

My only thought was hoping like nothing else that my heroic skills would come back. I didn't care if I was lucky or fluky or whatever, and I didn't care one bit if I got a reward, I just wanted to help save Johnny's family's stuff. A plan formed in my mind.

It was a daring plan.

It was a brave, courageous plan.

It was a crazy, risky plan.

It was a plan I had to actually do or the robber would walk off while I was lying on the ground thinking about plans. I got up, picked up my bike and wheeled it to the road. I swung my leg over and took a deep breath. It was time to put the plan into action.

CHAPTER NINE

My plan was simple. I would ride my bike quietly up to the ladder. I would get off my bike. I would pull the ladder out from underneath the robber. He would fall to the ground and be knocked unconscious. The Police would come and take him away. There were no accidents planned, which I guess is why they're called accidents.

I rode as quietly as I could. The robber continued slowly down the ladder. He stepped down another rung. I got off my bike and lay it on the ground. He still didn't know I was there. I sneakily snuck over to the ladder, careful not to stand on a stick or something to give myself away.

I was fine.
I got to the ladder. The robber
was only three rungs from
the bottom! He could
basically just step off
backwards now. And
that's what he did.
What he **didn't** do
was **not** crash
into me. He

actually did that quite well, and
knocked me over. He wobbled,
overbalancing with the bag.
The back of his foot bumped
into me as I lay on the ground,
and he started to fall.

NooOooooO!!

I cried out, as he
fell towards me. It didn't stop him falling. He let go
of the bag and it landed right next to my head. *He*

landed right on top of me, knocking the wind out of me in a gush. It gushed right into his face, in fact.

'Orrrrrrrrrrrrrrrrrr,' he groaned, rolling off me as fast as he could.

I remembered I had eaten leftover garlic prawns for breakfast. I sat up and looked from him to the bag. He looked from me to the bag. My eyes narrowed. His eyes narrowed. I was closer, but he had the advantage of being a ruthless robber.

I stood up in a crouch. My fingers twitched, ready to grab the bag and start running. He crouched and his fingers twitched, ready to grab the bag and start running.

'Alright kid,' he said, 'Time to help me out again. Third time lucky hey?'

'Nope,' I answered, ready to move. 'Third time blucky.'

Blucky? Really? Damn, a real hero would have thought of something witty. His eyes narrowed even further.

'Blucky's not even a word,' he said.

I knew that, but tried to pretend it was.

'Is so. We learnt it at school.'

We hadn't really. I was covering up.

'I mean, come on, kid' the robber said, standing up straight, distracted now. 'There are **heaps** of rhyming words you could have used.'

I straightened up too.

'Are not.'

'Are too,' he said. 'I mean, you could have breathed on me again and said third time chucky. Because trust me, I would have chucked up. Your breath is rotten!'

That was okay, I guess. I needed to say something smart back.

'But I was saying that not only was I not going to help you, I was going to take the bag **and** stop you getting away. Blucky. Take that, Sucka.'

Yeah, real smart and witty. He countered.

'Well, you could have said third time sucky.'

'What if I got something out of the bag and threw it at you?'

'Third time ducky.'

'Only if I wanted you to duck.'

'No, you would have grabbed a china duck. It's on the top of the pile.'

Oh.

'What if it was a china chicken?' I asked.

'Third time clucky.'

'A china horse?'

'Third time bucky.'

'Glue?'

'Third time stucky.'

'An ice hockey stick?'

'Third time pucky.'

What was this guy, a rhyming dictionary?

'Fine,' I said. 'You win. Take the stupid bag. Make a getaway. See if I care.'

As I finished speaking, a car pulled into the driveway. I turned to look and stood on the end of a rake. I fell and the rake flipped up and hit the robber right between the eyes. He cried out in pain, his hands flying to his face. I grabbed the china duck out of the bag and threw it at him.

It missed, and hit the windscreen of the car.

The cracked windscreen meant the driver, Johnny's dad, drove straight onto the lawn and over the robber's foot. He yelped and hopped around. He hopped on the rake, it flipped up, hit him on the nose, and knocked him out.

Johnny's mum called the police. The robber started to wake up. Johnny got out of the car and jumped on his back. I ran over to help. As I did, the robber twisted and started getting out from under Johnny. I took another step.

I stepped on an old rotten banana, which was all squishy and gross, and I went flying. Luckily, I came down hard, and my butt landed right on the robber's head and squashed it into the ground.

And that was how the police found us. Me sitting on the robber's head. Johnny on the robber's back. Rotten, stinky banana all over my shoe.

I rubbed my shoe on the grass to try and get the grossness off, but I accidentally rubbed it on the robber's face just as he was coming to. Stinky rotten banana went up his nose and in his mouth. He groaned and passed out.

Anyway. What that crazy scene meant was that the robber got arrested and all the stuff stolen from Johnny's house was safe. Except for the china duck. That, and the windscreen of Johnny's dad's car, were smashed. Johnny's dad said it was alright. And then he said something else.

'Jackson, you were in the right place at the right time. You're a hero.'

That was the best thing I had heard anyone say in a long time ... well, in a few days at least. Nan and the giant dream cupcake sun had been right. Once I accepted who I was, that my flukiness was a gift, and that it was a good thing to help for the sake of helping, everything changed.

I was back.

I was

ACCIDENTALLY AWESOME

again!

ABOUT THE AUTHOR

As a child, **Adam Wallace** dreamed of being a zombie hunter, a ninja warrior, or a Collingwood football player.

None of these things happened, and he's glad because:

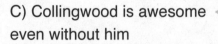

A) Zombies try and eat your brains and he probably would have died

B) Being a ninja warrior is really hard and he probably would have died

C) Collingwood is awesome even without him

D) He gets to write books and that is the best job he could ever *EVER* want!!!

Find out more about Adam at www.adam-wallace-books.com

ABOUT THE ILLUSTRATOR

Born with a pencil and paper in his hands **James Hart** was soon raised on a healthy balance of comics, video games and cartoons.

Once he realised that you could do drawings as a job he set forth on a journey of becoming that guy that draws stuff in books.

James' most favourite things to draw are aliens, monsters and robots.

Check out more of James' drawings at www.jameshart.com.au

OTHER STUFF BY ADAM WALLACE

Rhymes with art

Better out than in

better out than in Number twos

The Pete Mcgee Trilogy

jamie brown is not rich

Random

OTHER STUFF BY JAMES HART

BOY VS BEAST SERIES

YOU CHOOSE SERIES

GLENN MAXWELL SERIES

THE DAY MY BUTT WENT PSYCHO
(TV SERIES)